T.R. Bear

T.R.'s FESTIVAL

Terrance Dicks
Illustrated by
Susan Hellard

Piccadilly Press · London

For Valerie Bierman

Text Copyright © Terrance Dicks, 1987

Illustrations Copyright © Susan Hellard, 1987

Phototypeset by V.I.P. Type Ltd., Milton Keynes, Bucks.
Printed and bound by R. Hartnoll, Ltd.,
Bodmin, Cornwall.

for the Publishers, Piccadilly Press Ltd.,
15 Golders Green Crescent, London NW11 8LA, 1987

British Library Cataloguing in Publication Data

Dicks, Terrance
T.R.'s festival,—(T. R. Bear).
I. Title
832'.914 [J]   PZ7
ISBN 0-946826-88-9

Other books in the series
T.R. BEAR – ENTER T.R.
T.R. BEAR – T.R. GOES TO SCHOOL
T.R. BEAR – T.R.'s DAY OUT
T.R. BEAR – T.R. AFLOAT
T.R. BEAR – T.R.'s HALLOWE'EN
T.R. BEAR – T.R.'s BIG GAME
Terrance Dicks is the producer of the BBC TV Classic Serial.
He is well-known for his children's books,
including his novelisations of Dr Who.
Piccadilly Press publish his *Ask Oliver* series,
The Adventures of David and Goliath series,
and *The Camden Street Kids* series.
He lives in the Hampstead area of London.

Susan Hellard is a popular young illustrator. Among the books she
has illustrated for Piccadilly Press are: IT'S NOT FAIR,
JUST A MINUTE, UGLY DUCKLING, BILLY GOATS GRUFF,
and the *Dilly* series.
She lives in the Crouch End area of London.

Chapter One

Mystery on the Night Train

They were on their way.

Even now, Jimmy couldn't believe it was really happening.

It was almost midnight, and he was tucked up in bed, T.R. Bear on the pillow beside him.

Nothing unusual in that, you might say.

But the bed was a British Rail bunk, the bedroom was a little sleeping compartment, and they were thundering along the rails towards Scotland at goodness knows how many miles an hour.

Even the snores of his brother George from the upper bunk couldn't spoil the romance of it all.

George had no sense of adventure, but Jimmy was too excited to sleep.

His parents were presumably sleeping too, in the next compartment. His sister Jenny had a compartment to herself in the next carriage.

T.R. Bear was wide awake. He jumped up and went to the window, raising the blind a little.

Jimmy caught a glimpse of lights flashing past in the darkness, and thought of all the people asleep in ordinary, everyday beds.

T.R. lowered the blind. "Long way to go yet, kid. We're still just outside London."

T.R. wasn't supposed to come to life when there were other people about. But George was so sound asleep he didn't really count. Besides, George was so stuffy he wouldn't believe in a walking, talking teddy bear even if he saw one.

Jimmy settled back on his pillow with a contented sigh.

T.R. Bear trotted back along the

bed and sat down on the pillow beside him. "Gimme the lowdown on this festival again, kid."

"Every year they have a big arts festival in Edinburgh – theatre, opera, painting, ballet, everything. And every other year there's a book festival as part of the big one."

"Right, gotcha," said T.R. "And that's where your old man's going?"

"That's right. You know he writes history books for kids – you helped him to sell the first one, remember?

Well, he's written a whole series by now and they're doing so well he's been asked to speak at the book festival first thing tomorrow morning. He had to lecture at the college today, so the only way to get there in time was to travel overnight."

And thank goodness for that, thought Jimmy. A train journey to Scotland was exciting enough, but a journey that actually started at bedtime was even better.

T.R. was even more pleased and excited than Jimmy. "You know something, kid, I've always wanted to go to Scotland. You might say I've got ancestors there."

"You, T.R.? I thought you were an all-American bear!"

"Sure I am. But most people in

the U.S. of A. came from over here originally, you know. Though in this case, it's the other way round."

By now Jimmy was thoroughly muddled and said so.

T.R. said, "You remember how us teddy bears originally got started? President Roosevelt was out hunting and he ran across this bear cub."

Jimmy nodded. "He said it was too small to shoot and let it go. Someone drew a cartoon about it in the paper, and someone else, someone with a toy shop, made a toy bear and called it Teddy's Bear. What's all that got to do with Scotland?"

"Well that first teddy bear was so popular that the toy shop guy made lots more. Lots of Americans had

relatives back in Scotland, and the story goes that quite a few of those early teddy bears were sent over as presents." T.R. sighed. "Gee, it sure would be an honour to shake paws with some of those old-time guys!"

While T.R. was talking Jimmy realised he was going to have to get out of bed.

The little sleeping compartment had almost everything you might need, beds, a place to hang clothes and even a mini wash-basin. The one thing it didn't have was a toilet, and whether it was excitement or the coke he'd had on arrival on the train, a toilet was what Jimmy needed.

Explaining the situation to T.R., Jimmy clambered out of bed, got his dressing-gown from the end of the bunk and his slippers from under it and put them on.

With T.R. sitting on the pillow, he opened the door cautiously, so as not to awaken George.

Leaving the door ajar, he padded off down the darkened train-corridor, brushing past a dressing-gowned man who was coming in the opposite direction.

A few minutes later, Jimmy himself came back down the corridor, slid open his compartment door and went inside, closing it behind him.

He could hear rattling snores, coming from George in the upper bunk.

"We'd better get some sleep, T.R.," began Jimmy, and then broke off.

Peering through the gloom, he could see only the whiteness of the pillow and the grey British Rail blanket.

T.R. Bear had disappeared.

Chapter Two

Kidnapped!

At first Jimmy wasn't all that worried.

Since T.R. could move about when he wanted to, it seemed quite likely he'd just moved to some other part of the compartment.

But he hadn't.

Jimmy switched on the light – George groaned and turned over but didn't wake – and searched the entire compartment.

Since the whole place wasn't much bigger than a cupboard it didn't take long.

T.R. wasn't there.

Switching off the light, Jimmy sat down on the end of his bed and thought hard.

T.R. *might* have wandered off down the corridor – but it didn't seem likely. Even T.R. had too much sense to move about where he risked being seen.

So if he hadn't gone off of his own accord, T.R. must have been taken off. Kidnapped – or was it bearnapped?

With a guilty pang, Jimmy remembered he'd left the door open. Anyone could have picked up T.R. from the end of the bunk.

Suddenly Jimmy realised who must have done it.

The Fat Man!

They'd noticed him on the platform earlier on, a big fat man in an expensive-looking leather jacket, smoking a big cigar.

He was marching along the platform in a lordly way, a porter carrying two big suitcases staggering along behind him.

He'd made a huge fuss about finding his compartment and getting settled in.

They'd bumped into him again in the corridor – his sleeping berth

was just a few doors down from
theirs.

Since he was so bulky, they'd had
quite a job to squeeze past him.

Suddenly, the Fat Man had
noticed T.R., whose head and
shoulders, as usual, were poking
out of the school bag over Jimmy's
shoulder.

Quick as a flash, the Fat Man had
snatched T.R. out of the bag,
holding him up to examine him.
"What a lovely old teddy bear," he
boomed in a rich fruity voice. "May
I ask where you got him?"

Jimmy didn't like the way the man had snatched up T.R. without asking – he thought it was pretty rude to say the least. Not for the first time, he thought that there was a huge fuss if children were rude to adults, but when adults were rude to kids no-one seemed to care.

Even Jimmy's mother didn't seem to think there was anything wrong. "He is nice, isn't he? He was a present from some relatives in America. Jimmy's quite devoted to him."

She spoke in that special tone parents use when they talk about their kids in public, and Jimmy squirmed.

Worse still, the Fat Man patted Jimmy on the head with a big, damp hand. "Getting a bit old for a teddy, aren't you, old chap?" He leaned over Jimmy confidentially. "You probably don't realise, but an

old teddy bear like this in good condition is worth quite a bit to a toy collector. What would you say to fifty pounds?"

Jimmy's father gasped. "Fifty pounds!"

Reaching up, Jimmy snatched T.R. back and stuffed him into the school bag. "I'm sorry but T.R. isn't for sale!" With that he'd ducked into his sleeping berth.

The Fat Man had chatted to Jimmy's parents for a bit longer, pouring on the oily charm. He tried to persuade them to persuade Jimmy to change his mind, then, realising it was no good, stumped off to his own compartment.

"He even hinted he'd raise his offer," said Jimmy's father when he popped in later. "We told him it was no use though. Who'd have thought old T.R. was worth so much money!"

As he sat on his bunk in the gloom, Jimmy remembered all this and felt sure he knew what had happened.

The Fat Man had come along the corridor just as Jimmy had left – Jimmy suddenly remembered the bulky dressing-gowned shape that had brushed past him.

That must have been the Fat Man. He'd come along the

corridor, seen T.R. on the bunk and hadn't been able to resist snaffling him. Jimmy felt so sure that he decided there was only one thing to do – go and get T.R. back.

He marched along the corridor and hammered on the door of the Fat Man's berth.

At first there was no answer but Jimmy just went on banging. Finally a sleepy voice muttered, "All right, all right!"

The door opened and the Fat Man appeared, looking enormous in a bright yellow dressing-gown. He also looked cross.

"Well, what do you want?"

"I want my teddy bear back, please."

"What teddy bear?"

"The one you took off my bunk just a few minutes ago."

"I did no such thing. If you've lost your toy, little boy, there's no use your coming crying to me about it!"

He tried to shut the door, but Jimmy jammed himself in the doorway.

"Oh no you don't," he yelled. "You took my bear and I want him back. You were after him earlier, and when I wouldn't sell him you decided to pinch him instead!"

"How dare you accuse me of stealing!" bellowed the man. "I am a world-famous expert on toys, and I'm going to the festival. Do you think I would stoop to steal your miserable old bear?"

"Yes, I do!" shouted Jimmy.

By now they were making so much noise that doors were opening all along the corridor, including that of Jimmy's parents.

"What's happening?" asked Jimmy's father.

Jimmy explained, and his father looked grave. "Did you actually see this gentleman take T.R.?"

"Well, no," admitted Jimmy. "But he passed me in the corridor – at least, someone passed me and I'm

pretty sure it was him. The door
was open, T.R. was on the end of
the bed and he'd have gone right
past him."

"You see?" said the Fat Man.
"There is no proof, no proof at all.
Anyone could have come by and
taken the toy."

Suddenly, Jimmy noticed
something.

There was a small suitcase on the
luggage rack above the Fat Man's
bunk. It was rocking to and fro –
and it was rocking much more
violently than you'd expect from

the movement of the train.

Deliberately Jimmy raised his voice. "I know T.R.'s in here and I want him back!"

The suitcase rocked more violently than ever.

"I refuse to be insulted like this!" shouted the Fat Man. "Have a care, little boy – "

The suitcase gave a final rock, and rocked itself clear out of the luggage rack.

It bounced off the bunk, crashed down to the floor and burst open – and there was T.R. Bear!

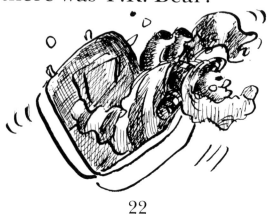

Chapter Three

Teddy Bears' Picnic

Jimmy jumped forward and snatched up T.R., hugging him tight. "See!" he said triumphantly.

Jimmy's dad glared fiercely at the Fat Man. "Well?"

"Oh, *that* bear," said the Fat Man immediately. "I found it lying in the corridor a little while ago. The boy must have dropped it there. I put it in my case for safety. I was going to hand it in when we got to Edinburgh."

It was an unconvincing story to say the least, and Jimmy just knew the Fat Man was lying.

But he also knew that there wasn't much they could do about it. No-one was going to get very excited about a stolen teddy bear, especially when the bear had already been returned.

He tugged his father's sleeve. "Never mind, Dad, we've got T.R. back and that's all that matters."

The fuss died down, and everyone went back to bed.

Back in their bunk with George still snoring away above them Jimmy whispered, "Well done, T.R.!"

"Well done yourself, kid! The

guy snaffled me right off the bunk the minute you'd gone. Soon as I heard your voice I started jumping around in the case. That guy's a crook, kid, we've gotta keep an eye on him!"

"Never mind," said Jimmy consolingly. "We'll probably never see him again!"

But Jimmy was wrong.

Next morning, after what seemed like a very few hours' sleep, they all arrived in Edinburgh very early in the morning.

They got a taxi to their hotel. It was quite a short ride and Jimmy, peering sleepily out of the window, got a quick impression of a long wide street with big shops on the right. On the left was a large garden area with lawns and flower beds, and beyond that a story-book castle on top of a rocky hill.

The taxi turned off to the right and drove into a big square, drawing up outside a posh-looking hotel.

"Here we are," said Jimmy's father. "Here's our hotel – and there's the book festival!" He pointed to the square which was filled with enormous tents.

They checked into their rooms – Jimmy was sharing with George again – and went into the hotel dining room for a splendid breakfast.

Then they crossed the road and went into the square. The book festival was open now and people were pouring through the gates of the square, wandering in and out of the various tents and up and down between them.

They had a quick look round the festival and found that most of the tents had been fitted up like giant book shops, with rows and rows of books of every kind.

There was a splendid refreshment tent too. It was more like a building than a tent inside, with glass mirrors and polished wood everywhere, wooden booths to sit in and a round wooden dance floor in the middle.

Yet another tent had been fitted up as a meeting hall with rows of

seats and a platform and desk for the speaker.

It was here that Jimmy's father gave his talk – the opening event of the day.

He was very nervous at first, but as the talk went along and his modest jokes all got laughs he gained confidence. He gave a spirited and amusing talk on why history didn't have to be boring,

and why children's history books really mustn't be.

At the end of the talk there was a big round of applause, and lots of people gathered round to ask questions and congratulate him.

After the talk they went back to the refreshment tent to celebrate. Jimmy's mum had collected a lot of leaflets and brochures about other events at the Festival and they all started planning how they wanted to spend the rest of the day.

It soon turned out they all wanted to do different things. His father wanted to stay at the book festival and listen to the other talks, his mother wanted to go to an exhibition of Chinese pottery, his sister Jenny wanted to go to the art gallery and brother George was keen on listening to some music in the square.

"Sounds as if we'd all better split up," said Jimmy's father. "We can meet back at the hotel for supper. What about you, Jimmy? You've got your pocket money and we've studied the map, so you know your wayaround."

Hurriedly Jimmy said, "Oh, I'll just wander about for a bit and see what turns up."

His mother pressed a leaflet on him. "There's a toy museum up in the Old Town. It says here they've

even got a special exhibition of teddy bears."

"There you are then," said George teasingly. "You can take T.R. He might find some long-lost relatives."

Before very long, Jimmy and T.R. were wandering through the busy streets of Edinburgh. Or rather Jimmy was wandering. T.R. as usual was riding in Jimmy's school bag, his head poking out of the top so he could see what was going on.

There was plenty to see. The streets were full of people up for the Festival and nearly all of them seemed to be in costume or make-up, or carrying some kind of musical instrument.

"Looks to me like everybody's in

some kinda show," rumbled T.R. "If everyone's up on stage, who's gonna be in the audience?"

"Maybe they take it in turns," suggested Jimmy. "How about we go and see the Castle?"

They had a wonderful time exploring Edinburgh Castle, and Jimmy decided to try and persuade his parents to get tickets for the famous Military Tattoo.

When they came out they ran across some Scottish dancing in a little square, and when that was over they found a little cafe and had fish and chips, Jimmy slipping coke and chips to T.R. when no-one was looking.

What with one thing and another the afternoon soon went by, and it was nearly time to think about going home.

Jimmy took a look at the leaflet his mother had given him. "Let's take a look at that toy museum," suggested Jimmy. "It's not far away, and there's just time for a quick look round before it shuts."

"Fine by me, kid. Maybe that smart-aleck brother of yours is right and I'll find one of my Scottish ancestors there." Earlier T.R. had

insisted in looking in one of the
shops that sold tartans to tourists.
They had a special chart on the wall
so you could see which clan you
belonged to.

Jimmy was sure T.R. was just
longing for a kilt and sporran and
one of those round hats with a
bobble on top.

"I'm afraid there doesn't seem to
be a Clan MacBear," he teased.

The toy museum was in the High Street – it had been set up in what had once been an ordinary house. "Only half an hour till closing time," said Jimmy. "Still, there's time for a quick look round."

It was certainly a wonderful place, filled with toys of every possible kind.

One room was filled with all kinds of bikes, from old-fashioned bone-shakers to the most modern BMX. There were scooters and miniature cars and trolleys too, everything with wheels. Above was a room filled with model trains and model cars.

Most interesting of all for Jimmy and T.R. was the dolls gallery.

Not so much because of the dolls (though there were all sorts there, from old ones in beautifully-made costumes to the most trendy modern kind), but because of the bears.

In the big display case at the end was a teddy bears' picnic, attended

by bears of every kind. There were bears sitting around tucking into realistic looking food, a bear in a deck chair, a bear resting on a towel under an umbrella, and even a bear riding on an elephant.

Watching over them was the biggest bear Jimmy had ever seen. "Willya look at that!" gasped T.R. in admiration. Jimmy guessed that for T.R. it was like meeting all your ancestors.

Suddenly, they heard heavy footsteps behind them.

Jimmy glanced round and saw a massive figure coming into the gallery.

It was the Fat Man – the man who'd tried to steal T.R. on the train!

Chapter Four

T.R's Army

Jimmy moved hurriedly away from the teddy bears' picnic, pretending to be interested in a display of dolls nearby. But the Fat Man didn't seem to recognise him. Indeed, as far as Jimmy could tell he didn't even see him. He was staring greedily at the teddy bears in the case.

He looked at them for a moment longer, then turned and went up the stairs that led to the gallery above.

A voice from below called, "Closing time. The museum will be closing in five minutes!"

The few people left in the dolls gallery went off down the stairs, followed by a handful of others who came down the stairs from the gallery above.

"We'd better be going," said Jimmy a little uneasily.

"Forget it, kid," whispered T.R. fiercely. "We don't go until *he* goes – the fat guy up there."

"What do you mean? Why not?"

"Don't act dumb, kid. Fatso's a thief, right? He even tried to steal *me*! And here he is lurking about next to some of the most valuable teddy bears in the world."

"You think he's going to try and steal them?"

"You can bet on it, kid."

Jimmy was horrified. "We've got to go and tell the museum people!"

"Tell them what? We've no proof, the guy hasn't done anything yet."

"So what do we do?"

"We wait here and catch him in the act – " T.R. cocked his head. "Quick, hide!"

Jimmy ducked down out of sight behind a display case in the corner.

A lady came through the gallery and went on up the stairs.

After a few minutes she came down again. She switched off the lights and went downstairs.

"Checking the place is empty before she locks up," whispered T.R.

Jimmy nodded. "Lucky she didn't see us."

"She didn't see Fatso either," pointed out T.R. "Betcha the guy came here earlier and cased the joint, found himself a hiding place. Soon as the coast is clear he'll come down, then we'll grab him."

"*We'll* grab him? He's a lot bigger than either of us – than both of us put together, come to that."

T.R. rubbed his chin with a paw. "You're right – we gotta get help."

"Where from?"

T.R. jumped out of the school

bag. "You leave that to me. Take a look upstairs, see if you can spot the fat guy without him spotting you. If he starts coming down, pop back and warn me."

Jimmy hurried across to the stair, but he couldn't resist turning back to see what T.R. was up to.

T.R. marched across to the teddy bears' picnic and rapped upon the case with his paw. "Wake up in there, you guys. We gotta major

crisis on our hands!" The bears didn't move. "Now don't play dumb with me," pleaded T.R. "I know the rules say you can't come to life with humans about, but this is an emergency . . ."

Jimmy hurried up the stairs and peered through the doorway of the gallery above.

It seemed to be some kind of waxwork display, with life-like figures wearing the costumes of different ages.

But there was no sign of the Fat Man, and there didn't seem to be anywhere he could hide.

Then suddenly one of the model figures moved – and Jimmy suddenly realised it *was* the Fat Man.

He was wearing a floppy black coat that looked something like a cloak, and he had a black hat pulled down over his eyes. In the shadowy room he was just a massive black shape amongst the other models.

As Jimmy watched, the huge black figure turned its head and started moving slowly towards the door.

Jimmy turned and scurried down the stairs. "Look out, T.R. – I think he's coming!"

T.R.'s voice came from somewhere in the shadows. "Okay, kid, hide in the corner behind that case – and stay outta the way.

Fatso's in for a big surprise!"

Jimmy shot into the hiding place and waited. Seconds later he heard stealthy footsteps coming down the stairs.

The Fat Man appeared in the doorway – and gave a sudden gasp of surprise.

Jimmy gasped too, even more astonished than the Fat Man.

The teddy bears' picnic case was empty.

The deck chair, the towel, the picnic things, even the elephant were all there, but the bears had gone.

The Fat Man rushed over to the case and stared in amazement.

A voice behind him said, "Okay, Fatso, the game's up!"

The Fat Man whirled round.

T.R. stepped out of hiding and stood glaring up at him.

The Fat Man loomed over him. "So, it's you!"

"You bet your life it's me, buster. And I know all about your crooked scheme."

"A teddy bear that can move and talk," said the Fat Man softly. "You will be worth more than all the others put together. I shall take you!"

"Oh no you won't, Fatso!"

"And who will stop me?"

Jimmy was about to go to T.R.'s
help when a chorus of growly voices
said, "We will!"

A ring of teddy bears stepped out
of the shadows, surrounding the
Fat Man.

Leading them was the giant bear.
With a ferocious growl, the huge
bear advanced on the Fat Man, the
others following . . .

The Fat Man gave a yell of panic and headed for the stairs that led to the exit.

T.R. dashed to the stairs to stop him and the Fat Man tripped over him and rolled down the stairs with a tremendous crash. A minute later Jimmy heard him rattling at the front door and yelling, "Keep them off me! Let me out! Let me out!"

Suddenly alarm bells began to ring . . .

*   *   *

"And that was that," concluded Jimmy. He was back at the hotel, explaining to his astonished family just how he and T.R. had arrived back at the hotel in a police car. "Somehow he set the burglar alarms off. Luckily there was a police car passing, and the museum lady had just that minute left. She let the police in and they carted him away and then brought us back here."

There was quite a lot that Jimmy wasn't telling of course.

Like the way the Fat Man had been babbling about bears coming to life so the police thought he was potty.

Or the way that next time Jimmy had looked at the case the teddy bears had all been back at their picnic – though they did look a bit ruffled and they weren't in exactly the same places as before.

Jimmy wondered if anyone would notice.

"It sounds like quite an adventure," said his sister Jenny.

And his brother George said, "And did T.R. get to meet any of his ancestors?"

Jimmy looked at T.R. who was sitting in an armchair pretending to be just an ordinary teddy bear again.

"You know, I rather think he did," said Jimmy slowly. "In fact, you might say it was quite a family reunion!"